CW01459236

TULLY AND
THE TUMMY ACHE

Available in the Tales of Tully series

Tully's Life
This heart-warming story follows the journey of Tully from street dog to much-loved family pet, teaching young readers about the importance of kindness, understanding and hope.

Tully Takes Off!
Tully has arrived in her new home with her new grown-up, but she does not like it one bit! When Tully sees an opportunity to go back to her old life on the streets - the only life she has known up to now - she takes it with both paws. With a search underway, it is up to her new grown-up to work out what Tully needs and help get her safely home.

Tully and the Sad Day
Tully has woken up feeling grey and cloudy inside and she does not know what to do. She cannot help her big feeling because she does not know what it is. As her different feelings begin to work together in the wrong way, it is up to Tully's grown-up to help her to understand what she needs.

Go To Sleep Tully!
It is night time and Tully is tired, but she does not want to go to sleep. Her new grown-up knows that Tully is trying every trick she can to avoid going go to bed! With lots of adventures planned and Tully needing her rest, Tully's grown-up needs to find a way to help Tully learn to not be so worried about bedtime.

Tully and the Midnight Feast
Tully is a newly-adopted dog settling in with her new grown-up. Since her arrival, her snacks have started mysteriously disappearing from the cupboard and appearing under her bed, she seems to have forgotten her manners, and there are days when she just cannot stop eating! Tully and her grown-up need to work together to help Tully with her worries about food.

Tully and the Scary Day
Tully has woken up feeling scared. She isn't really sure why, but today feels like a very scary day, and she just wants to hide. Tully's grown-up is thankfully there to help Tully manage her big feelings and see that the day is not so scary after all.

Don't Touch Tully!
Tully is settling in with her new grown-up. She has learned that the new grown-up is a safe person and she enjoys strokes and cuddles with them. Then Tully starts to meet new people, who want to show her how loved she is. Unfortunately, Tully doesn't feel the same about people she does not know and trust. It is up to Tully's grown-up to find a way to help Tully with her big feelings and to be Tully's voice, when she can't use hers.

Tully and the Tummy Ache
Tully has a tummy ache and it's making her feel quite grumpy. She doesn't want to eat or drink, and she can't get comfortable. Her tummy is sore and it's getting worse! Tully is in a toilet muddle. So, Tully and her grown-up work together to sort the muddle out and help Tully to cure her tummy ache.

Tully's Birthday
It's Tully's birthday, and her grown-up has planned a special day for her, but Tully doesn't feel like celebrating. As the day begins to unfold, so do Tully's big feelings. Tully doesn't know what to do about the big feelings, so she does a bad thing. Luckily, Tully's grown-up is there to help her feel better about herself, and enjoy the rest of her birthday.

Listen, Tully!
Tully does not always like to listen, especially when her grown-up is trying to stop her having fun. Tully decides that instead of listening, she can be in charge. But when things start to go wrong, Tully and her grown-up need to work out how Tully can begin to find listening a little bit easier.

Tully and the Makeover
Tully has been having lots of fun playing in the mud, but now her grown-up says she has to have a bath. Oh dear! Tully is not sure she wants one of those. She is feeling a bit nervous about what is going to happen to her, but Tully's grown-up shows her that there is nothing to worry about. Having a bath is a good thing after all.

Tully and Vera
Tully has moved in with her new grown-up but she is missing her foster carer, Vera. Tully is struggling to understand why she had to leave, and whether it is okay to have big feelings about Vera. It is up to Tully's grown-up to try and help her to understand loss and endings and why, sometimes, they have to happen to make space for new beginnings.

Tully and the Chase
Tully loves to be chased. It gives her a feeling of excitement which starts off as being fun, but one day the excited feeling suddenly and very quickly becomes a feeling which is too big. Instead of feeling excited, Tully starts to feel scared. Tully and her grown-up need to work out how they can play Tully's exciting game without it becoming a bit too much for her, and causing a muddle.

Tully at Christmas
Things are starting to feel a bit different in Tully's house and all around outside. Tully's grown-up looks different, strange lights are appearing everywhere and people have started putting their gardens indoors! Tully is not sure what to make of this thing called Christmas – she just wants everything to stay the same. What can Tully's grown-up do to make Christmas-time a nicer time for both of them?

Tully Goes on Holiday
Tully has gone on a holiday with her grown-up. After a difficult start, things seem to be going well. But when the fairground opens up, with all its flashing lights, loud music and food smells, Tully's big feelings get the better of her, making her want to run. And she does! Tully's grown-up needs to find her in time to show her that holidays can be fun after all.

Tully and the New Rules
Tully likes lots of things about living in a house with her grown-up, but one thing she really doesn't like is all the rules! Tully thinks the rules are all very boring and her grown-up must want to stop her from having fun. One day Tully breaks her least favourite rule, and something bad happens. Tully doesn't know what to do! Can Tully's grown-up get to the bottom of this muddle so it doesn't happen again?

Tully and the Tummy Ache

TALES OF TULLY

Jess van der Hoech

Trauma Tools
& Training

Copyright © 2024 Jess van der Hoech
All rights reserved.
No part of this book may be reproduced in any form or by any electronic or mechanical means, including information storage and retrieval systems without permission in writing from the author, except by reviewers, who may quote brief passages in a review.
The individuals and organisations mentioned in this book are included with their permission, and do not constitute a recommendation or endorsement of the services they provide.
ISBN-13 978-1-06-86917-2-0
Editing by Sarah Ogden
www.jvtraumatools.co.uk

Acknowledgements

As always, to my trusted editor Sarah Ogden for all that you do to make these books come to life. I will never fully know what goes on behind the scenes, but it is a joy to work alongside you on these projects. Thank you.

Thank you to my supervisor Linda Hoggan for your continued support, encouragement, discussion and much-welcomed feedback on this series. I learn so much from you and the knowledge I have gained form our conversations has been invaluable across my practice, the books and now this series. Thank you.

Thank you to Laura Benham, for your support in giving me feedback, the searching questions, your friendship and of course, the countless conversations about dogs, the content of which has become quite useful! Thank you.

To the children and families who I meet in my therapy room, from whom I have learned more about hope and healing than any course could ever teach me. Your input, ideas, questions and answers are so valuable to me and I will be forever grateful. Thank you.

Preface

The *Tales of Tully* series is based on the adoption of an ex street dog from Bosnia who came to live with me in September 2023. Watching her try to settle and adapt from everything she had previously known to fit in with a new way of life began to present a number of ideas as to how to communicate such difficulties that can be experienced, to others who are in the process of adopting or who have adopted children. The aim of the series is to provide an opportunity to explore different situations, circumstances, feelings and experiences, finding new ways of communicating and understanding each other, through the voice of Tully.

When Tully first came to live with me, she did not urinate for almost four days. I was with her in the garden for hours at a time, but she was persistent in her refusal to use the toilet. It made sense to me; she was terrified of marking her territory, because she did not know where her territory was. She simply did not feel safe. In the end, her body made the decision for her and eventually the toilet was produced, much to my relief, as well as hers! The fact it was on the kitchen floor did not matter at that stage, it was better that than a trip to the vets for antibiotics when she would inevitably become unwell from holding her bladder for so long.

She held on for her bowel to move for almost a week, and even following this, was not going as often as she should. I would notice a change in her behaviour; she would become quite erratic, unsettled, her body movements would be jerky and she would be reactive to any little noise. It took me a while to make the connection that there was nothing really 'wrong' with her, she just had a very full bowel that she was struggling to hold.

By addressing this with her and making toilets safe, rewarding her with her favourite chest rub when she went, the connections were made and she started doing what her body wanted to do, rather than trying to resist.

Using the toilet properly can be a big issue for many children who have experienced early trauma. Infrequent bowel movements have been linked to feelings of anxiety, beyond the 'bowel shyness' of using a strange loo. The longer it is held, the more scary it feels to go, because the child knows that by that point, it may physically hurt to use the toilet. It is a cycle which continues until the body can hold on no longer, sometimes leading to embarrassing mishaps and subsequent feelings of shame.

In my therapy room, I have previously worked with a number of children who have been prescribed a high dose laxative to counteract this problem. The holding of the bowel movements was assumed to be caused by anxiety, which led me to ask the question, "what exactly are they anxious about?" In some cases, there had been a history of early trauma, and nappies had sometimes been an issue. I began to wonder whether the inability to use the toilet was part of the generalised anxiety in the child, or could it be linked specifically to anxiety around using the toilet?

'Safe toilets' became part of the work I was doing with children and upon exploring their big feelings, past and present, we began to melt the toilet muddles and the prescription laxatives could be stopped. The children I worked with responded well to using Tully's voice to find their own, to explore a subject that is often linked with feelings of embarrassment and shame.

How to use this book

First and foremost, ensure that both you and the child are well-regulated and comfortable when you begin to read Tully's story. Make sure you choose a time when you are unlikely to be interrupted. The child may like a soother, a favourite or fidget toy, a drink or something to suck or chew to help them to stay regulated.

If the child is calm, then begins to try and distract or move away from the reading, make a note of what they have just heard in the text. It is very likely that they will have just provided you with some valuable information about something that they cannot tolerate or want to avoid for now.

The questions have been designed not only to explore the internal world of the child, but to help to develop a common language between the child and adult who are using this book together. The child cannot get the answers to the questions incorrect. Their interpretation of the thoughts and feelings Tully is having may provide some very significant information about the child's own thoughts and feelings. The child may want to expand the answers to talk about themselves and may even be able to make comparisons between Tully's feelings and their own.

Tully and the Tummy Ache

Jess van der Hoech

Tully could not get comfortable. She had tried sitting and lying in lots of different ways – on the sofa, on the floor, sitting up, lying down – and still she was restless.

Can you draw Tully?

When Tully was uncomfortable and restless, it could also make her seem a little bit grumpy. She wasn't grumpy though. Tully knew what was wrong; her tummy hurt.

What other feelings might Tully have?

Tully had no energy. She had not had anything to eat or drink because her tummy hurt too much, and now she was tired and hungry too. It felt like a very bad day.

"Come on Tully, toilet time!" her grown-up said, and took her into the garden.

What might Tully do now?

Tully was not very happy about being taken into the garden because she did not want to go to the toilet. In fact, that was the reason her tummy hurt – because she would not go to the toilet.

Tully was in a muddle.

What might Tully be thinking?

When Tully was very young, she had lived on the streets in Bosnia all by herself. She was a 'street dog'. This meant that she did not have a grown-up to take care of her.

When she had been a street dog, Tully had to learn a lot of things by herself. She did not always get it right.

Once, Tully saw a dog going to the toilet on the street.

"Aha! That's what I should do!" Tully thought. She used the toilet in the same place.

Was this a good plan?

How might Tully have felt about learning to use the toilet here?

What else could Tully have done?

When a dog uses the toilet somewhere, they are telling the other dogs "This is my place! Stay away!" but Tully did not have anyone to teach her this. She was learning by copying.

The other dog saw Tully go to the toilet in his place and he became very cross with her and chased her away!

How might Tully have felt when the dog chased her?

Another day, Tully found another place to use the toilet. She found a patch of grass that did not smell of any other dogs.

"I can use the toilet here," Tully thought, so she did.

Unfortunately, Tully had gone to the toilet in someone's garden and they were not pleased at all. They came outside and shouted at Tully.

How did Tully feel when the grown-up shouted at her?

How does this make Tully feel about using the toilet?

Tully had moved into a shelter in Bosnia with her foster carer and lots of other dogs. It had taken a while for Tully to learn that it was safe for her to go to the toilet there.

How might Tully be feeling now?

When Tully moved to the UK with her new grown-up, she had been very scared and frightened about everything. Tully did not want her grown-up to shout at her, and she didn't want to get into any trouble, so she made a plan. Tully would not use the toilet at all!

Is this a good plan?

What would happen if she did not use the toilet when she needed to?

What else might Tully be worried about her grown-up doing?

For several hours after she arrived in her new home, Tully did not go to the toilet. She held on…and on…and on…and on. Tully held on until her body could not hold on anymore and – oh dear! During the night, Tully wet her bed.

How is Tully feeling about this?

Tully did not know what her grown-up would do and she felt frightened. In the morning, Tully hid behind a chair. She did not want her grown-up to see her.

"Good morning Tully, it's a beautiful day!" her grown-up said.

Tully stayed quiet. She had big feelings inside her but she did not know what she should do.

Tully could hear her grown-up busy in the kitchen. She heard the washing machine start. Then, her grown-up came back with some fresh, clean bedding.

How is Tully feeling now?

"Go to the toilet Tully" her grown-up said, letting her out of the back door and into the garden.

Tully remembered the person shouting at her when she went to the toilet on the grass in Bosnia. She had not liked that at all. Tully thought this grown-up might shout at her too, so she did not want to go to the toilet on this grass either. Tully was in a toilet muddle.

Can you draw or write about Tully's toilet muddle?

What does Tully need?

Every few hours, the grown-up took Tully into the garden and said "Go to the toilet Tully."

After a few trips outside, Tully had a think. She wanted to eat and drink but she couldn't because of her hurting tummy. Tully was with a new grown-up who was asking her to go to the toilet. When she had wet the bed, Tully had not been in any trouble. Maybe her new grown-up wanted to help?

Tully was still worried but decided that the next time the grown-up told her to go to the toilet, she was going to. The next time they went into the garden, Tully used the toilet.

What do you think happened next?

A Celebration! "Good toilet Tully!" her grown-up said and gave her a chin scratch which Tully loved. The grown-up told Tully she was a "clever girl." Tully liked hearing good words about herself.

"I know it was difficult for you before to know what you were supposed to do," her grown-up told her.

"I know when you need to go to the toilet, because I notice that you get a grumpy feeling. I know that you must be worried about going to the toilet because your tummy feels painful too."

"You will never be in trouble with me for going to the toilet, and when you go when you need to, your tummy won't hurt anymore."

You know what to do now, you can be the boss of your body and go to the toilet when you need to."

How does Tully feel about what her grown-up has told her?

What worries, if any, might she still have about going to the toilet?

The next time Tully was let into the garden, she went to the toilet without being asked. Tully felt very proud of herself.

From then on, every day she went to the toilet when she needed to. Tully's grown-up was very pleased with her.

No more toilet tummy aches for Tully!

About the author

Jess van der Hoech is a qualified therapist who has spent the last ten years studying and working with the impact of developmental trauma and, in particular, the assessment and treatment of children and adolescents with complex trauma and dissociation.

As well as supporting birth families, Jess works with looked-after and adopted children and families, using skills in attachment-focused therapy and therapeutic parenting techniques.

Jess is a supervisor, trainer and motivational speaker with a passion for writing therapeutic books that are accessible to children and families to help with the healing process and to increase awareness in the impact of trauma.

Jess van der Hoech

Also by Jess van der Hoech

What A Muddle (2016) ISBN 978 18381987 0 1 (Co-authored with Renée Potgieter Marks)
An interactive, practical workbook designed to help children who have difficulties with emotional regulation to begin to understand what is happening in their bodies. A variety of activities throughout the book enable the child to start to explore these ideas through the story of Sam, while gently encouraging them to begin to verbalise their own experiences. Carrying out the physical exercises in the book can promote changes in emotional regulation. The text is written in a child-friendly, gender-neutral style, and is easy to understand for parents, carers and practitioners alike. For children aged 4-12.

These Three Words (2018) ISBN 978 18381987 5 6
Also available as an e-book. A unique therapeutic novel for teenagers with the aim of linking together the feelings, emotions and behaviours connected to anxiety, with some of the therapeutic tools that can be used in order to enable better self-regulation, increased confidence and different ways of thinking. The book is equally valuable to parents of teenagers with anxiety, giving them an insight and understanding into some of the issues that may be affecting their child, and potentially opening up a line of communication and a way forward between parent and teen.

These Three Words: The Journal (2019) ISBN 978 18381987 2 5
A thought-provoking and hands-on workbook, combining a series of practical exercises and tools designed to assist teenagers who are struggling with the symptoms of anxiety. Addressing the anxious responses in both brain and body, this journal provides the reader with the opportunity to discover therapeutic coping techniques and learn how to apply them to their own personal problem areas, before committing to a twenty-eight-day practice to promote good emotional regulation and reduced anxiety. The journal can be used alongside the therapeutic novel These Three Words, or as a standalone workbook, and it is suitable for use by the teenage reader on their own, with a parent, or in a group.

Beastie, Baby and the Brand-New Mummy (2022) ISBN 978 18381987 3 2 and *Beastie, Baby and the Brand-New Daddy (2022) ISBN 978 18381987 4 9*
A therapeutic story that looks at the external signs of pathological dissociation in a child. Dolly's story helps children who have experienced early trauma to begin to understand, in a very simple way, what dissociation is and why it has happened in their internal world. Tools and techniques are included within the story that parents and caregivers can use to assist the child in the first stages of their healing process. Beautiful illustrations on every page enhance the story of Dolly, and help the reader to relate to the events that happen, to notice the methods Dolly has developed to manage her feelings, and to think about what is happening in their own internal world. For children aged 4-12

Printed in Great Britain
by Amazon

62815522R00025